Greta Gorsuch

KEY CITY ON THE RIVER

Greta Gorsuch has taught ESL/EFL and applied linguistics for more than thirty years in Japan, Vietnam, and the United States. Greta's work has appeared in journals such as *System*, *Reading in a Foreign Language*, *Language Teaching*, *Language Teaching Research*, and *TESL-EJ*. Her first book in the Gemma Open Door Series is *The Cell Phone Lot*. Greta lives in beautiful wide West Texas and goes camping whenever she can.

First published by GemmaMedia in 2019.

GemmaMedia
230 Commercial Street
Boston MA 02109 USA

www.gemmamedia.com

Printed in the United States of America

978-1-936846-79-5

Library of Congress Cataloging-in-Publication Data

Names: Gorsuch, Greta, author.
Title: Key city on the river / Greta Gorsuch.
Description: Boston MA : GemmaMedia, 2019. | Series: Gemma open door |
Identifiers: LCCN 2019005491 (print) | LCCN 2019006510 (ebook) | ISBN
9781936846801 (ebook) | ISBN 9781936846795
Classification: LCC PS3607.O77 (ebook) | LCC PS3607.O77 K49 2019 (print) |
DDC 813/.6--dc23
LC record available at https://lccn.loc.gov/2019005491

Cover by Laura Shaw Design

Map courtesy of Library of Congress, Geography and Map Division. https://www.loc.gov/resource/g4150.ct002299/

Gemma's Open Doors provide fresh stories, new ideas, and essential resources for young people and adults as they embrace the power of reading and the written word.

Brian Bouldrey
Series Editor

GEMMA

Open Door

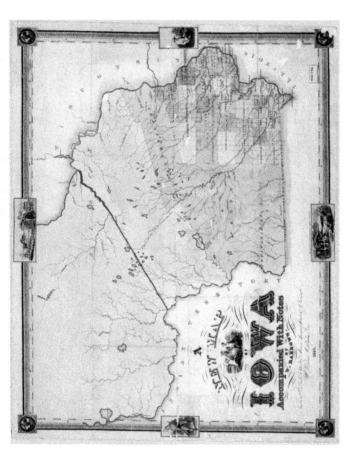

CHAPTER ONE

Illinois, The mouth of the Fever River,
November 21, 1833

"Penny! Nate! Where are you?" called Mr. Butterman. "Ella! Where did those two go?" he asked his wife, Mrs. Butterman.

"I saw them over there," said Ella Butterman. She pointed to the water's edge. She said, "Let Aunt Sunday find them. She knows where they are."

Mr. Butterman walked fast over to Aunt Sunday. He was in a hurry. They had to get started. It was getting late in the day. It got so dark, so fast, in November.

Aunt Sunday was sitting on a log not far away. She looked at the small Fever River on her left. It was like a thin rope. It curved into the distance, back to Leadville. That's where they came from this morning. Then she looked at the huge Mississippi River straight ahead. That's where they were going. And they weren't just going *to* the Mississippi River. They were going to *cross* it. Aunt Sunday never saw such large river. There was so much water in it! She could hear that dark water rushing by. She was old, and she couldn't hear well. But she could still hear that river making noise. She didn't want to go. There was a new home across that river, in the new Iowa Territory. But she didn't care. She felt very, very far from home. Once she crossed the Mississippi, she thought she might never go home to Virginia again. So when she heard Mr. Butterman shouting for Penny and Nate, Aunt Sunday stayed quiet. Then Mr. Butterman came to her saying, "Aunt Sunday! Help me find Penny and Nate!"

"Yes sir," said Aunt Sunday. It sounded like she said *Yasshuh*. Her voice had a soft sound. Aunt Sunday only had three teeth left due to age. And she spoke how she learned back in Virginia. She got off the log slowly. She was a small woman. Her hair was white. She turned around slowly. Then she pointed. There they were. Penny was throwing a stone into the fast water. Nate was just watching that river with all that water go by. "Over there," she said. It sounded like she said *Ovatheah*.

"You two!" shouted Mr. Butterman. "Get over here!" Aunt Sunday watched Penny and Nate turn around and slowly walk back over the hard ground. When Nate got near enough, Mr. Butterman jumped closer. Then he grabbed Nate's shirt collar and pulled him along faster, back to the two wagons. Penny stayed far enough away from Mr. Butterman. He was in a bad mood from waiting. "Best to let him cool off," she thought to herself. She went to Aunt Sunday and walked with her to the wagons. It was time to cross that river. It was time to go.

CHAPTER TWO

Illinois, The mouth of the Fever River,
November 21, 1833

Mr. and Mrs. Butterman, Aunt Sunday, and Penny and Nate got into the two wagons. Mr. Butterman drove one wagon and Nate drove the other. Two horses pulled each wagon. Mr. Butterman's riding horse, Harv, was tied behind Mr. Butterman's wagon. Harv was a tall dark brown horse, restless from the deep water he saw ahead.

They waited in line behind a family with three wagons. They were going to cross the Mississippi River on a small ferry. The ferry, a small flat boat, could only take two wagons at a time.

The owner of the ferry had four men. When someone wanted to cross the fast, dark water, they got on the ferry at the Illinois side of the river. The ferryboat owner and the four helpers then paddled the boat to the Iowa side of the river. On each side of the river, there was a ferry landing. This was where people, horses, and wagons got on or off the ferry. On the Iowa side, the landing was at the base of a bluff. This was a tall, very steep hill with rocks and trees. At that part of the river, steep bluffs rose on each side.

Another thirty minutes went by. Mr. Butterman waited and waited. He talked to himself. Sometimes Mrs. Butterman would say, "Yes, dear."

And then Mr. Butterman would begin talking to himself again. He thought the ferry crossing was taking too long. It would be dark soon. It was very cold. The late afternoon November light was a thin blue. In the second wagon, Nate looked at Penny. She smiled and lifted one shoulder up. She was tall. She wore a long, dark striped dress and an old pair of boots from Mrs. Butterman. She had a warm shawl around her shoulders that she made herself. She knew how to sew by hand. She made many clothes for Mr. and Mrs. Butterman. She smiled with her dark lips, showing white teeth. She had skin the color of dark tea. But her hands and nose were red from the cold. She asked Nate, "Do you know how to swim?"

"Yeah," he said. "But we may not need it today!" He took Penny's hand. He held her hand for a few minutes. His hand was warm. Penny gave him her other hand to hold, too.

"I hope not," she said. "There's a lot of water in that river." She turned to Aunt Sunday, who was very, very quiet. "Aunt Sunday?" she asked. Aunt Sunday didn't answer. Penny looked at Aunt Sunday more closely. Aunt Sunday had her eyes tightly closed. She was talking to herself. "Aunt Sunday?" Penny asked again.

"Can't talk now," said Aunt Sunday, keeping her eyes closed.

The Buttermans' wagons pulled up to the ferry landing on the Illinois side. The ferry owner Jones and his men got the two wagons, Harv, Mr. and Mrs. Butterman, Nate, Penny, and Aunt Sunday onto the ferryboat. They pushed away into the Mississippi River.

CHAPTER THREE

On the Mississippi River
between Illinois and Iowa
Territory, November 21, 1833

Things were fine until they got close to
the Iowa side of the river. Here the river
was deeper, and it ran faster. The sun was
going down. And the tall bluff ahead
made it even darker. The sun was set-
ting behind it. The trouble began with
Harv, Mr. Butterman's tall riding horse.
Harv was never good with water. He
didn't like this deep, fast water at all.
He began to pull at his rope at the end
of Mr. Butterman's wagon. Nate quickly
got off his wagon. Mrs. Ella Butterman
saw this. She was always quick-thinking.

She tossed Nate a large piece of cloth. Nate tied the cloth over the horse's eyes so he could not see the water. Harv got a little quieter. Then suddenly, a very large log crashed into the side of the ferryboat. The log was really a large tree floating in the water. Aunt Sunday cried out in the back of the wagon. She was scared.

Jones the ferry owner shouted, "It's all right! There was a storm a few days ago! There are lots of trees in the water today. Don't worry!"

But Harv didn't care what the ferry owner said. With the crash of the log on the side of the boat, he went wild. He pulled on the rope as hard as he could. Suddenly, the rope snapped free. Harv fell over the side of the boat into the deep, fast water. Nate ran to the side of boat. Harv's head came out of the water. Nate grabbed Harv's rope. He held Harv's head above water. It was hard to hold on to Harv. He was such a large, strong horse. Mrs. Butterman ran over to help. So did Mr. Butterman. "Hold him!" yelled Mr. Butterman. The water was fast, but just then they got to the edge of the river. Harv's feet found the rocky river bottom.

It was almost dark now. Harv climbed up out of the river. Nate jumped out of the boat after him. He held onto Harv's rope. He led the wild horse away from the water onto the muddy riverbank. Mr. Butterman drove one wagon off of the ferryboat. Mrs. Butterman climbed onto the second wagon. Penny moved over and Mrs. Butterman sat next to her. Mrs. Butterman drove the second wagon off the boat. Then she turned to Aunt Sunday, who was crying into her shawl.

"Aunt Sunday," she said. "You're going to be all right. It's over. We're across. We're in Iowa."

But Aunt Sunday just cried. Ella Butterman turned to Penny. Penny said, "She told me this morning she didn't want to cross the water. She thought she would never see Virginia again if she crossed the Mississippi."

"Ah," said Mrs. Butterman. "Well . . . I'm sure she misses home." Mrs. Butterman herself was from Ohio. She had never been to Virginia. "So what do you think, Penny? What do you think about Iowa so far?" she said.

Penny answered, "I can't really see it! It's too dark!" Both women laughed softly.

Nate tied Harv to the back of Mr. Butterman's wagon. Harv was shaking and cold. Nate climbed into the wagon next to Mr. Butterman. The two wagons rode into the darkness. They would camp tonight. But tomorrow they would be in Key City.

CHAPTER FOUR

Iowa Territory,
November 22, 1833

Mrs. Ella Butterman woke Penny up. The sun was not yet up. But the sky in the east was a thin blue with a bright, bright star.

"It's time to make breakfast," said Mrs. Butterman. "Mr. Butterman wants to get started early. He wants to get to the Land Office in Key City. Maybe find the land we bought."

"Yes, alright," said Penny. She sat up. She wrapped her shawl tightly around her. It was so cold, much colder than Maryland, where she was from. Penny climbed out of the wagon. She tied on her warm boots. She called to Mrs. Butterman, "Should I wake up Aunt Sunday?"

Ella Butterman answered, "No. She's tired out from crossing the river yesterday. Let her sleep. She can start cooking again tomorrow." Aunt Sunday was the best cook Penny ever saw. But if she needed a rest today, then so be it. Penny walked over to the fire. The sun came over the edge of the earth with a flash of red, then gold. The sky got bright. The bright star in the east faded away.

Penny fried some meat over the fire. Mrs. Butterman found some cold biscuits from yesterday. She boiled coffee. She said, "Mr. Butterman is hunting for our dinner. He should be back soon. I hope he gets a turkey." As soon as she said that, she heard a gunshot, far away. There was another shot. Then a third shot. Then the sound faded. Penny smiled. Mr. Butterman talked a lot. And he worried a lot. He felt he never had enough time. But he was good with a gun. Whenever he shot his gun, he hit what he pointed at. So if that was his gunshot just now, they were going to have fresh meat for dinner.

Iowa Territory was new territory. It had opened to white people only the year before. Before that, it was Indian territory. Only Indians could live there, west of the Mississippi River. The Indians, the Sauks and the Foxes, had many villages. It was their home for hundreds of years. But times changed.

White people wanted the land. And so many people like the Buttermans quickly made plans to go to Iowa Territory. They bought land. They made plans to farm, to mine for lead, or to open a business.

But this life was not going to be easy. Key City, where they were going, was less than a few months old. There were no shops. There were no banks and no churches. There was nowhere to buy meat. There were no roads, really. There were just some Indian trails. There were only a few houses. Instead there were deep, dark forests. There were many small rocky streams and rivers. These were filled with fish and turtles. There were many animals. Penny could see two or three deer standing back in the shadows of the trees. If you wanted fresh meat, you could hunt for it.

Breakfast was ready. Mrs. Butterman saved a plate of food for Mr. Butterman. Penny called Nate to come for breakfast. He was taking care of Harv. The big riding horse had cuts on his legs. The rocks in the river were hard on Harv's legs. Lucky for Harv, Nate knew what to do. He had some special medicine and he gently put it on Harv's cuts. Nate was good at doctoring horses and other animals.

"Come on to breakfast, Nate!" called Penny. Nate left Harv and came to the fire.

CHAPTER FIVE

Iowa Territory,
November 22, 1833

Mr. Butterman brought two turkeys from his hunting trip. He was smiling. "What luck!" he said. "This is good land. I saw five or six turkeys!" He put the turkeys on the cold ground. Then he sat down and ate his breakfast. He was done in less than two minutes. Like everything else, he did it fast. He drank some hot, strong coffee and walked over to Harv. He looked at Harv's legs. He called over to Nate, "Did you try your special medicine?"

"Yes sir," said Nate. It sounded like *Yassuh*.

"Hmm," said Mr. Butterman. "That looks good. You're good with Harv."

Nate's teeth flashed in a smile. "I learned to take care of horses when I was a boy."

"Where are you from?" asked Mr. Butterman. "I never asked."

"From Virginia, sir. The same place as Aunt Sunday," said Nate.

"Hmmm," said Mr. Butterman again. He said that when he was thinking about something. "Well," he said, "Let's get out of here. I want to find that land we bought. It might be a few hours away, still. My, it gets so dark so fast in Iowa!"

Penny woke Aunt Sunday up. She got the old lady a little breakfast. Then she and Mrs. Butterman quickly put out the fire. They got ready to leave. Penny could see the Mississippi River from the camp. But this side of the river seemed quieter. She couldn't hear the water as much. It was still a lot of water. But from here, in Iowa Territory, it seemed different. The sun coming up behind it turned the river into a huge golden rope. The biggest rope you ever saw.

Mr. Butterman tied Harv behind his wagon. He wanted to ride Harv, but Harv's legs had cuts on them. After a few days, Nate's medicine would begin to work. The two wagons drove north toward Key City.

They drove through thick trees. Sometimes the trees were so thick that it was dark under them. There was no road. It looked like a small path through the trees. At one place, a rocky bluff and the river came very close to each other. Penny thought her wagon would fall into the river. "Not again," she thought. But Mrs. Butterman was good with the wagon. They didn't have any trouble.

After an hour, they left the steep bluffs behind and they came to a flat area. It was very wet and muddy. Then they saw a small house. It was just a one-room log cabin. It didn't have any windows. Smoke came from the stone chimney. Then the single door of the cabin opened. A white woman looked at them. Mr. Butterman spoke to her. She answered, pointing to a path that went between two steep hills, off to the left. Then she went back into her house.

Nate turned around from the first wagon and looked back at Penny. Then Penny and Aunt Sunday looked at each other.

"That is one small house," said Aunt Sunday.

"It sure is," said Penny.

Aunt Sunday and Nate were from Virginia. There were large houses in Virginia, with many windows and doors. Penny was born in Maryland. They had large houses there, too. None of them ever saw a white person living in such a small house. Black people, like them, might live in small houses. But their owners, who were white, lived in six- or seven-room houses.

The wagons started up again. They headed up the path to Key City.

CHAPTER SIX

Key City, Iowa Territory,
November 22, 1833

Another hour went by. They climbed up
and down hills. They followed the nar-
row path. They started to see men working in what looked like small caves in the
rocky bluffs. There looked to be dozens
of small caves all up and down the bluffs.
The men stopped their work when they
saw the two wagons. They watched the
wagons go by in silence.

Soon Penny could smell smoke.
They came off the path and to a large
group of small buildings. The trees
were cut down in a large circle. Ten
or twenty buildings were grouped

inside the circle. This was Key City.

Key City was only three or four months old. The men who first came cut down as many trees as they could. They had to do it by hand. It was hard work. Then they used the trees to make log cabins. Most of the buildings were one- or two-room log cabins. But a few buildings were plain wood. The wood was a bright brown. It was new wood, and Penny could smell how fresh it was. The largest wood building had a sign that said "Land Office." She could see another wood building with the sign "Medical Doctor" on it. So Key City had a doctor. That was good.

Mr. and Mrs. Butterman got down off their wagons and went into the Land Office. Nate again looked back at Penny sitting in her wagon. He lifted his shoulders in the air. Penny laughed softly and nodded back. With only a few wood buildings, Key City could not really be called a city.

Some men came out of the log cabins to look at the Buttermans' wagons. Two of the men looked at Nate. Then they talked to each other. They were rough and dirty. Penny knew what trouble looked like. And these white men looked like trouble. Penny sat up straight on the wagon. This was not good.

The two men walked across the cold ground to the wagon were Nate was. One of them, a short man, said to Nate, "Whose wagon is this?"

"This is Mr. Butterman's wagon,

sir," said Nate. His voice was calm and quiet.

"Suh!" said the other, taller man. "Did you hear him say 'suh' or is that 'sir'?"

The men laughed. The short one went behind the wagon to look at Harv. Harv moved and pulled on his rope hard. Nate was out of the wagon faster than Penny could believe. He stood between Harv and the short, ugly man. The man was trying to untie Harv's rope. Harv did not like it.

"Sir," said Nate. Both men laughed loudly. Then Harv pulled his rope again. Very hard.

"Do not touch Mr. Butterman's horse," said Nate. Now his voice was louder. "Get back."

More people came out of the log cabins to look. The door on a small wood house opened up. Two white women came out. One of the women called out, "Are you stealing that horse, Mr. Ginn? Are you?" The two men stopped laughing. The woman was wearing a dark green dress. She had light golden hair. She came closer, picking her way over the hard ground.

CHAPTER SEVEN

Key City, Iowa Territory,
November 22, 1833

The lady in the green dress was small.
But the way she walked made her seem
tall. She said again, "Are you stealing
that horse? Well, Mr. Ginn? I heard
you had trouble with that in Illinois.
Stealing horses. That's why you came
here. Hmm?"

The shorter man, Rick Ginn, said
"Shut up, you . . ." Then he stopped.
He saw even more people coming out
of the log cabins, and the Land Office.
They were all looking at him. He
looked at the taller, dirty man. Then
he said, "Ed, let's get out of here," and

they moved away. They went into the woods at the bottom of a steep river bluff. People stood outside for a few minutes, talking. They watched the two men go into the forest. But it was too cold to stand outside for long. The lady in the green dress walked over. She said to Penny, "Hello! Where are you from?"

Penny answered, "We came with Mr. and Mrs. Butterman. There they are." She pointed. Ella and Jonathan Butterman came out of the Land Office and walked to the wagons.

Mrs. Butterman smiled at the lady in the green dress. They talked for a few minutes. The lady's name was Mrs. Wheat. The other lady was her sister, Miss Mallow.

Mrs. Wheat said, "Mr. Butterman, you should be careful. Rick Ginn and his brother Ed are interested in your horse, there. The Ginn brothers are horse thieves. Lucky for you, your man there," she pointed at Nate, "stopped them." Jonathan Butterman looked at Nate.

"Well, we thank you," Mrs. Butterman said to Nate. "And thank you, too," she said to Mrs. Wheat.

Mr. and Mrs. Butterman talked to Mrs. Wheat and Miss Mallow a bit more. Mrs. Wheat told them there were about two hundred people in Key City. Most of them were men. "They're mostly mining lead," she said. "It gets pretty loud at night. The men mine during the day and drink whiskey at night. We don't really go out."

Miss Mallow said, "But we're hoping to start a school, soon. There are a few families with children here. We had more families here last August, but . . ." she stopped talking.

Mrs. Wheat looked at her sister. "What my sister wants to say is that we had a lot of sickness just a few months ago. A lot of people died."

Mr. Butterman asked, "What kind of sickness?"

Mrs. Wheat answered, "Cholera. From the water."

Everyone was quiet for a minute.

Miss Mallow said, "But no one's been sick for a few months. It's fine now. Just be careful where you get your drinking water from."

"Yes," said Mrs. Butterman quietly. "Of course."

CHAPTER EIGHT

Key City, Iowa Territory,
November 22, 1833

Mrs. Wheat and Miss Mallow gave the
Buttermans directions to the Buttermans'
land. There weren't any roads. So, Mrs.
Wheat's directions sounded like, "Go
twenty minutes until you come to two
log cabins. That way. There will be a large
rock on the left. A tree is growing out
of the rock. Keep going. Then you will
see a bluff without trees. There are five
or six lead mines at the bottom of the
bluff. You will be able to see the mine
entrances clearly. Then you will come to
a small stream that is flowing towards

the Mississippi. That is Calder Creek. Cross Calder Creek and turn left. You will follow that for ten minutes. Then you will see a small stone house. That is where the Calders live. A nice German family. Your land is just five minutes past their house."

"A stone house?" asked Mrs. Butterman, surprised.

"Yes!" said Miss Mallow. "Mr. Calder is very good with stone. He built it in only three months. If you want a stone house, I'm sure he can help you."

"I would like that," said Ella Butterman. "There's a lot of good stone here."

Mr. and Mrs. Butterman got into their wagons and said goodbye. They drove off in the direction that Mrs.

Wheat told them to go. Aunt Sunday spoke up from the back of the wagon. She said, "Lucky those two white ladies came by." Neither Penny nor Mrs. Butterman answered.

The directions from Mrs. Wheat were right. They saw the rock with the tree growing out of it. Then they saw the steep bluff with lead mines at the bottom. The entrances looked small and dark. Three men came out of one mine with buckets of dark rocks. "Lead?" thought Penny.

They came to Calder Creek and crossed it. Then they came to the Calders' house. The two wagons stopped. A red-haired man came to meet them.

"Yah?" he said.

"I'm Jonathan Butterman," said Mr. Butterman.

"Oh yah! Butterman! We're waiting for you!" said Mr. Calder. "Good! Good!" he said. It sounded like he said *Gut! Gut!* Then he pointed. "Just past there. That is your land." He walked ahead and the two wagons followed.

All Penny could see were trees. So many trees. She saw Calder Creek on her left. It was a faint silver rope of water. She thought she saw rocky hills, or bluffs, on the right. But there were so many trees she couldn't be sure.

Mrs. Butterman said, "Trees, trees, and more trees." She sighed. "Well, we're home."

CHAPTER NINE

The Buttermans' land on
Calder Creek, Iowa Territory,
December 20, 1833

November and December stayed warm.
Nate and Mr. Butterman quickly built a
two-room log cabin with trees they cut
down. Every day Mrs. Butterman and
Penny spent an hour collecting large
rocks from the Buttermans' land. They
made a large pile near the log cabin.
Mrs. Butterman wanted an extra room
for the house built out of stone. "Maybe
in March or April," said Mr. Butterman.
"I want to get something built for the
horses first. I think the weather might
turn cold soon." He and Nate found a

spot on the Buttermans' land that was perfect. It was a rocky area against the bottom of a short bluff. They made a rough building for their four workhorses and for Harv. During the winter, the horses would stay warm.

On some days, Mr. or Mrs. Calder would visit. Sometimes Mr. Butterman would give them a turkey or part of a deer he shot. And sometimes Mr. Calder helped collect rocks for the extra room Mrs. Butterman wanted. Once, Mrs. Calder brought fresh eggs. In return, Aunt Sunday made a cake from the eggs and some cornmeal and sugar she had. "This is good Virginia cooking. Cornbread," she told Mrs. Calder. Mrs. Calder, a lady with blonde hair, spoke only a little English. So Aunt Sunday said again, "Cornbread." Mrs. Calder nodded and smiled.

There was another farm ten minutes away from the Buttermans'. Penny could smell the smoke from their fire. But she never saw anyone.

Today, Mr. and Mrs. Butterman said it was a rest day. They gave Penny and Nate a free afternoon. So Penny and Nate went to see the other farm. They followed Calder Creek for twenty minutes. Finally, they found two small log cabins under the trees. To Penny's surprise they saw a woman and two children. All three were dark-skinned, just like her and Nate. Penny and Nate came forward to say "hello." The women looked around and then said "hello" back. The two children, a boy and a girl, looked to be eight or nine years old. They came close and said "hello." Penny found out the woman's name was Alice. The little boy and girl were hers. They were Charles and Teeny. They were twins.

Alice kept looking around into the trees. Penny asked her, "Are you alone here? Are you alright?"

Alice answered, "This is Mr. Sweeney's place. There's him, and then there's Bowe and Tommy."

At that moment, Penny heard a rough man's voice. "Alice! Where are you?" A hard-looking man with white hair and blue eyes came out of the forest. He was followed by two dark-skinned men, one of them very tall. "Who are you and what are you doing here?" said the old man. His blue eyes flashed. "Get off my land!" he said. His white face grew red. Alice, Charles, and Teeny melted away without a sound. They went into one of the log cabins.

Nate moved closer to Penny. "Sir," he said, "We're Nate and Penny. We live at the Buttermans'." He pointed back to the Buttermans' land.

"Then you should get back there!" said Mr. Sweeney. "Does your master know you're gone?"

"I'm sorry, sir," said Penny. She stood very straight. What was wrong with this man? She didn't want trouble. "We're leaving now," she said. Nate and Penny turned and walked away. As they left, Nate smiled and waved at the two black men. One of them waved back.

CHAPTER TEN

*The Buttermans' land on
Calder Creek, Iowa Territory,
February 9, 1834*

It was a cold and snowy winter. The warm weather of late November held until Christmas. Then it snowed and snowed and snowed. Every day was cold and gray. Aunt Sunday stayed inside most days. She said the cold wet made her bones feel old. "It wasn't like this before we crossed the Mississippi," she said.

"Oh, Aunt Sunday," said Mrs. Butterman. "It was, too! Don't you remember being in Kentucky last year?

When we came to get you after Mrs. Morris died?"

"Yes ma'am," said Aunt Sunday. "It snowed a little. But Iowa feels cold. Just *cold*."

Mrs. Butterman said, "Perhaps you need a warmer shawl. I think I brought another one. Let me look." And she went into the other room of the two-room log cabin they all lived in together. She found the extra shawl. "Penny," she said.

"Yes, Mrs. Butterman?" said Penny.

"This old shawl came from Mrs. Morris," said Mrs. Butterman. Penny knew the shawl. She made it for Mrs. Morris the year before she died. It was black and gray and blue, and very large and warm. Mrs. Morris felt the cold so much in the last year of her life. Penny wrapped it around old Mrs. Morris to keep her warm.

"Yes ma'am," said Penny. "It was hers."

"Well," said Ella Butterman, "It's so large. Could you cut it to be smaller? Perhaps we can get an extra shawl for Aunt Sunday? And Mr. Butterman needs a scarf to put around his neck."

Penny took the shawl from Mrs. Butterman and looked at it. She said, "I think we could get a second scarf out of it, too. Nate gets pretty cold when he's out looking for wood."

Mrs. Butterman agreed. "Yes, you're right." And Penny got to work. Soon Aunt Sunday had an extra shawl for her small shoulders. Mr. Butterman and Nate had new neck scarves. For the next few months, they wore them every time they went outside. Aunt Sunday stopped talking about how cold she was. She sat by the stone chimney, where the fire burned. It was warm there.

Mr. Butterman made visits to Mr. Sweeney. He wanted to have a good neighbor in Mr. Sweeney. But Mr. Butterman was also worried about Mr. Sweeney's hard words to Penny and Nate. He was also curious about Bowe, Tommy, and Alice and her two children. He wondered if Mr. Sweeney owned them. Jonathan Butterman wasn't sure where owning slaves would go in Iowa Territory. Missouri to the south had slavery, but Illinois to the east had less. Owning slaves was a topic that interested a lot of people in the new Iowa Territory. But it was hard to discuss openly. Some people from Missouri, Kentucky, Virginia, or Maryland felt it was alright to own people with black skin. They needed slaves on their farms. But some other people from Ohio or New York were turning against owning slaves.

Mr. Butterman learned that Mr. Sweeney was from Missouri. And he owned his five "people," as he called them. Mr. Butterman stopped asking questions about that. He did, however, tell Mr. Sweeney that Nate was good with horses. If he ever had trouble with horses, Nate would help. For money to Nate, of course. Mr. Sweeney seemed surprised. Pay money to a black person? But he was happy to know someone could take care of his horses. He had two.

CHAPTER ELEVEN

*The Buttermans' land on Calder Creek,
Iowa Territory, April 18, 1834*

It was April now. The cold weather gave
way to warm sunshine. The snow melted.
The sky was a rich blue. Penny felt better now about Iowa Territory. She could
work outside in the sunshine. She helped
Mrs. Butterman collect large stones from
Calder Creek. She sewed clothes for Mr.
and Mrs. Butterman, and Nate and Aunt
Sunday. Mrs. Butterman brought a lot of
cloth with her from Ohio. She thought
that because Key City was only a few
months old, it might be hard to buy
cloth, food, and other goods. And she
was right.

Today, Penny just felt good. She was sewing a shirt for Mrs. Calder. Mrs. Calder had some chickens. With the warmer weather, she gave five baby chicks to Mrs. Butterman. By summer, they might have eggs! Because Penny's sewing was so beautiful, Mrs. Butterman gave Penny some blue cloth. She asked Penny to sew a pretty shirt with a collar for Mrs. Calder. Penny was happy to do so. In a few days she would be done. Then Penny and Mrs. Butterman would walk to the Calder farm. They would give Mrs. Calder the shirt. They both wanted to get away from the two-room log cabin and see something new.

Because Penny was outside more, she had more time to talk to Nate. On this day, Nate had Harv and the four wagon horses down by Calder Creek. Some early spring grass was up. The horses happily ate the new, fresh grass. Harv's legs were perfectly healed from his trouble in the Mississippi River. Nate's horse doctoring was good.

Penny and Nate talked for a while. Nate talked about his last visit to Key City with Mr. Butterman. "There are at least a hundred more people now," he said. "I can't believe how many log cabins are up. The people who built them worked all winter to do that."

Penny took Nate's hand. "I think we were lucky to get here last November," she said. "The weather was still warm then. There wasn't too much snow."

Nate laughed. "At least not until December. Then boom!"

Penny shook a little. She didn't want to think about that cold, snowy winter they just went through.

Suddenly, Harv stopped eating. He put his head up. His brown-black ears were straight up in the air. He really was a tall horse. Nate got up to see what Harv was looking at. "Hello," said Nate.

Bowe and Tommy, from Mr. Sweeney's land, came out of the trees. "Hello," said Tommy, the tall one. "H'lo," said Bowe. He was short and had big arms and a big chest.

Everyone was silent for a minute. Then Tommy said, "Don't tell Mr. Sweeney you saw us."

"Alright," Penny finally said.

Tommy said, "Mr. Sweeney thinks we're hunting. He won't miss us for a few hours. We can get as far as Key City in less than an hour if we keep walking fast."

Nate asked, "Where are you going?"

Bowe said, "Anywhere but here." It sounded like he said *Anwhea but heah*.

Penny sighed. Then said, "Well, goodbye then. Good luck."

The men waved. Then they disappeared into the trees. The last Penny saw them, they were headed away from Calder Creek. She guessed they didn't want the Calders to see them. They would get to Key City another way. Nate and Penny never told anyone.

CHAPTER TWELVE

The Buttermans' land on
Calder Creek, Iowa Territory,
April 20, 1834

Penny finished Mrs. Calder's shirt.
Jonathan Butterman said to Mrs.
Butterman, "Ella, you should ride
Missy and Lap." Missy and Lap were
two of their wagon horses. He continued, "They need the exercise. You can
ride Missy. Penny can ride Lap."

"Alright, dear," said Mrs. Butterman.
She liked the idea. There weren't really
any roads to the Calders' farm. There
was just an Indian trail next to Calder
Creek. It was still muddy from all the
winter snow.

A few minutes later, Ella Butterman and Penny rode along Calder Creek. The horses were happy to get out, too. As they got to the Calders' small stone house, they could hear shouting. "What in the world?" said Mrs. Butterman. Both women got off their horses and ran to the Calders' front door. There at the door Penny could see Mr. Sweeney with his white hair and angry blue eyes. He had his gun. He was shouting at poor Mrs. Calder.

"My two men ran off! Bowe and Tommy!" shouted Mr. Sweeney. "Have you seen them? They had to come this way! Bowe?! Tommy?!"

Mrs. Calder, who spoke little English, just looked scared. She was tiny next to this wild shouting man.

"Stop it!" said Ella Butterman. "Stop right now!"

Mr. Sweeney turned around fast. His surprise was so great it was funny. Penny almost laughed. Then she remembered Mr. Sweeney was holding a gun.

"What do you want?" said Mr. Sweeney, his face red and his eyes blue and hard as ice.

"I think a better question is, what do *you* want?" said Mrs. Butterman in a soft voice. "You are on the Calders' land. And you're scaring Mrs. Calder. She speaks little English. She probably doesn't know what you want."

"Oh," said Mr. Sweeney.

"Please put that gun down," said Mrs. Butterman.

"Oh," said Mr. Sweeney again. He lowered his long gun. "It's just a hunting rifle," he said.

"Mrs. Calder doesn't know that," said Penny, very quietly.

Mr. Sweeney looked hard at Penny. "I know you," he said. "You came on my land." He looked angry again. He said, "Don't you talk. I don't need to hear that talk from your kind."

"Ah, you must be Mr. Sweeney," said Mrs. Butterman coldly. "I heard about you. Now listen to me. Penny works for us. She's not a slave. We don't own her. And my husband and I are very lucky to have her help. So don't you call her 'your kind.'"

Mr. Sweeney just looked at Mrs.

Butterman, then at Penny. He couldn't say anything, he was so surprised.

"And her name is Penny Cooper," said Mrs. Butterman. Penny took a very deep breath. She had never heard Mrs. Butterman use her full name before. But Penny Cooper was her name.

"Perhaps you should just leave, Mr. Sweeney," continued Mrs. Butterman. "If you want to talk to Mrs. Calder about Bowe and Tommy, please wait until her husband is here."

Mr. Sweeney walked away fast, back to his land up Calder Creek.

CHAPTER THIRTEEN

Mr. Sweeney's land on Calder Creek,
Iowa Territory, April 20, 1834

After Ella Butterman and Penny got
home, Mrs. Butterman talked to her husband. She told him about Mr. Sweeney
and his gun. She told him how scared
Mrs. Calder was. Mr. Butterman gave
a big sigh. He needed to talk to Mr.
Sweeney. He needed to make him understand he couldn't scare his neighbors.
Even if his two slaves ran away, that was
not a good reason to shout at neighbors.

Jonathan Butterman walked up
Calder Creek to talk to Mr. Sweeney.
He went hunting the day before and
shot two turkeys. He carried one of the

turkeys with him as a gift. He walked until he could see Mr. Sweeney's two log cabins. He didn't think Mr. Sweeney was dangerous. But he did think Mr. Sweeney was old and maybe scared. He had to be careful as he got close to Mr. Sweeney's house.

Mr. Butterman saw Alice outside one of the log cabins. Her twin children, Charles and Teeny, sat on a log nearby. It was very quiet. Alice saw Mr. Butterman but said nothing.

"Alice?" called Mr. Butterman. "Is Mr. Sweeney here?"

"Yes he is, sir," said Alice. "But I'm afraid to go get him." She pointed to the log cabin against the rocky bluff on Mr. Sweeney's land. Mr. Butterman handed the turkey to Alice. She took it and said, "Thank you." She told the children to come closer. She wanted their help getting the turkey ready to cook. Their feet were bare even though it was only April.

There was nothing to do but go closer to Mr. Sweeney's house. Jonathan Butterman walked a little closer and then called, "Mr. Sweeney? Mr. Sweeney! Can you talk? Are you there?"

After a long minute, the door of the cabin opened. Mr. Sweeney appeared. He looked scared and tired. He said, "Tell your wife I'm sorry." Mr. Butterman waited. Then Mr. Sweeney spoke again. "With Bowe and Tommy gone, I don't know how I can live here. I need help cutting trees. I can't do it by myself. I just didn't think. I tried looking everywhere."

Jonathan Butterman said, "Nate and I can help. And I know some men in Key City who are tired of mining. They're looking for work. Do you want me to send them to you?"

Mr. Sweeney nodded.

"About Mrs. Calder," said Mr. Butterman, "I think you need to tell *her* you're sorry. You scared her. She doesn't speak much English. She didn't know what you wanted."

"Yes," said Mr. Sweeney. "Alright."

Mr. Butterman then said, "Anytime you need help, you can come to me. I don't know about Tommy or Bowe. I don't hold with owning people. But next time, talk to me first." Both men were quiet for a minute. Then Mr. Butterman said, "Maybe you can ask Tommy and Bowe to come back. They didn't get far, I'm sure. Maybe you can pay them. You won't have trouble if you do that."

Mr. Sweeney didn't answer.

CHAPTER FOURTEEN

The Buttermans' land on
Calder Creek, Iowa Territory,
May 19, 1834

Mr. Butterman and Nate spent most of April and May cutting down trees on the Buttermans' land. Sometimes they helped Mr. Sweeney, too. Mr. Butterman wanted to plant corn and vegetables as soon as possible. And for that they needed open land.

"I think the growing season here is short. If we plant now, we might get something before September," he told Nate. They cut trees all the way up to Mr. Sweeney's land. They cut trees all the way in the other direction down to the Calders' land. "Next year we can cut the trees up on the top of the bluffs there," Mr. Butterman pointed. He owned the land up there, too.

Mr. and Mrs. Butterman, Penny, Nate, and Aunt Sunday went out onto the newly cleared land. They used sticks to push holes into the ground. Into each hole they put three precious corn seeds. "One seed for me, one seed for you, one seed for the hole," said Nate. It wasn't the best way to plant corn. But they didn't have many tools. Penny said they ought to plant sweet potatoes. They had some sweet potatoes from last year. They could cut them up and plant them in the ground. Then they would have sweet potatoes to eat in August or September.

"Why sweet potatoes?" asked Mrs. Butterman.

"Sweet potatoes can help with summer fevers," said Penny. "You know, that fever from mosquitoes?"

"Yes ma'am," said Aunt Sunday. "There's nothing better than sweet potatoes for mosquito fever."

"Alright then," said Ella Butterman. "Let's plant them over there." She pointed to a sunny spot near Calder Creek.

Key City grew quickly after the warm weather came in. Mr. Butterman visited the small town once a week. He came back with reports. The winter was hard on people, he said. There were at least one hundred more people. But they were mostly lead miners. They were tough, rough men. They only brought their own supplies. They didn't have families. They just wanted to mine lead and take it back to Leadville to sell.

After one of those visits to Key City, Mr. Butterman talked with his wife about buying some more land. He wanted to build a house in Key City. "I know a good piece of land north of town. It's a lot closer to Key City than our land here on Calder Creek," he said.

"Why do you want to live in town?" said Ella Butterman. "There are so many mines. So many rough men. All that whiskey. Don't you remember the trouble we had with the Ginns? What if there are more like them?"

Surprised, Mr. Butterman looked at

Mrs. Butterman. She went on. "Penny, Nate, and Aunt Sunday might have a hard time. I don't think anyone really knows what is going to happen to . . . people like them . . . to people who were slaves. Is Iowa going to be free? Or is it going to have slaves?"

"I don't know," he said. "But I think we ought to live in town. We can't live being afraid of people like the Ginn brothers. And Penny and the others are free. They have papers. They can go where they like. We can give them money to go back to Illinois if they don't like it here."

Mrs. Butterman looked sad, but she said, "You're right."

CHAPTER FIFTEEN

*The Buttermans' land, Iowa Territory,
May 30, 1834*

To Mrs. Butterman's surprise, both Penny and Nate *wanted* to live in Key City. They were inside the two-room log cabin with bright sunshine streaming in the single door.

"We don't care about the Ginns," said Nate.

"And we . . . well . . . we want to say something," said Penny.

"Oh my. What is it?" said Ella Butterman.

Nate said, slowly, "Penny and I want to get married."

There were ten full seconds of

silence. Mrs. Butterman sat down quickly. Then she smiled, the biggest smile Penny ever saw. Mrs. Butterman said, "I don't know why I'm surprised. I see how you look at each other. Let me go and tell Mr. Butterman! He'll be happy to hear this wonderful news!" And she went outside to tell Mr. Butterman.

Later that day, Penny, Nate, and Mr. and Mrs. Butterman sat talking under a tree. Aunt Sunday was taking a little sleep.

"Nate and I can have our own house," said Penny. "I've been saving a little money from my sewing. And I've saved what you pay me. Nate has a little money, too. You know he's been doctoring the Calders' horses. Even

Mr. Sweeney asked Nate to doctor his horses. We can pay you rent."

Mrs. Butterman looked a little hurt. Penny said, "We're happy to stay with you and Mr. Butterman. But we spent all winter in the same rooms. Didn't you get tired of that?"

"Maybe a little," said Mrs. Butterman. "Although I grew up with my eight brothers and sisters in a three-room house in Ohio." Both women laughed. Then Mrs. Butterman asked, "Why didn't you two get married before?"

There was a very long silence. Then Mr. Butterman said, "Ella, my aunt, Mrs. Morris, was living in Kentucky. Remember, that's where we found Nate, Penny, and Aunt Sunday. They were my aunt's slaves. She owned them. That is done by some in Kentucky."

"Yes," said Mrs. Butterman, slowly.

"When Mrs. Morris died, she left all her land, her house, and her money to me. She left Nate, Penny, and Aunt Sunday to me."

Mrs. Butterman didn't answer.

"We could have married in Kentucky," said Penny. "There's no law against that. But if Mrs. Morris had wanted to, she could have sold any one of us. At any time. Even if I had married Nate and she wanted to sell him away to another family in another place, she could have."

Mr. Butterman continued, "Yes. That is why I had papers written up for your freedom. I thought that by coming to Iowa with us, then we, and maybe you, could start a new life."

Mrs. Butterman sighed. "Well, we all have a new life here. And Penny and Nate, I'm so happy for you! We need to find a priest to marry you. We'll ask Mrs. Calder. If she doesn't know, then we can ask the next time we go to Key City."

Everyone sat under the tree. They watched the whispering, silver water of Calder Creek.

CHAPTER SIXTEEN

The Buttermans' land, Iowa Territory,
June 5, 1834

Mr. Butterman found four pieces of land in Key City he wanted to buy. Three pieces were right in town, at the base of a steep bluff. The last piece was on the top the same bluff but a twenty-minute horse ride west, away from the river. "It's good farmland up above the river. Not so many trees," he said. "With our land on Calder Creek and this new land, we can sell corn or cattle within a few years." Mrs. Butterman thought this was a good idea. But she wondered where they would find enough help to farm all that land. Mr. Butterman had an answer for that. He said, "Not all the men coming to town want to mine lead. There are plenty looking for work in farming or in building. I also talked to Mr. Sweeney. He says he can work for a share of food from our farming. Our land here is close to his. It's not far for him to go. And he got Tommy back. Tommy can help out. I might be able to pay Tommy for work on our new land, too."

Mr. Butterman and Nate moved all the stones and rocks they gathered at Calder Creek. They had enough to start two small houses on the Buttermans' land in town. They would build a five-room house for Jonathan and Ella Butterman on one piece of land. The base of the house would be stone and the top part wood. Just five minutes away they would build a stone and wood four-room house for Nate and Penny. Penny would have an extra room for her sewing business. They would pay rent each month to Mr. and Mrs. Butterman.

Mrs. Butterman asked Aunt Sunday where she wanted to live. "What do you want to do, Aunt Sunday?" she asked. "You can live with Mr. Butterman and me if you like. We're happy to have you."

The old lady cook said less and less every day. Once it got warmer, she sat outside more. She sat by Calder Creek in the sunshine. She knew there was a big turtle there. She could see it lying on a rock in the warm sun. Its high, round shell was brown and green. On

those long warm days, Aunt Sunday lis-
tened to the sound of the water. She
knew the water went to the Mississippi
River. She knew that if she crossed
the Mississippi River back to Illinois,
she would be closer to her old home
in Virginia. She knew she would never
see Virginia again. She felt sad about
that. But if she did go, what life could
she have? She might not be free, not in
Virginia. But her childhood memories,
and her memories of being a young
woman, were sweet. Perhaps she just
wanted to be young again. She thought
those things as she watched the bright
edge of the creek slip by in the afternoon light. The big turtle made a splash
as it fell into the water and swam away.

Aunt Sunday never answered Mrs.

Butterman's question. But when the day came to move to the new houses, she wanted to stay with Mr. and Mrs. Butterman. She wanted her own room, just off the kitchen. She wanted a glass window. She had always wanted her own room with a glass window.

CHAPTER SEVENTEEN

Key City, Iowa Territory,
June, 1834

House building and wedding plans kept everyone busy in June. Mr. Butterman found a young man to build the stone parts of the two houses. His name was James Smith. He was a stone mason. He worked together with Mr. Calder, who knew German-style stone mason work. Within a few weeks, all the stone from Calder Creek was used up. Mr. Butterman now had the bases and chimneys for two fine houses. He could begin building the upper wooden parts of the houses.

Ella Butterman and Penny Cooper

asked Mrs. Calder about a priest. To marry Nate, Penny needed a priest. Mrs. Calder said, "I don't know. Maybe no priest yet?" But she said she would ask Mr. Calder. Then she said, "Wait here." In a few minutes she came back. She handed Penny a soft packet. "For your wedding," she said. Penny opened the packet. Inside was a beautiful pair of soft white gloves. "For your wedding day," said Mrs. Calder. "You will look beautiful!" Penny could hardly speak. No one ever gave her something so beautiful.

Mrs. Butterman and Penny went to Key City on Lap and Missy, the two wagon horses. They found where the two new houses were going up. Both Mr. Calder and young Mr. James Smith were working that day. James whistled a tune as he checked the stone base of Nate and Penny's house. He said a few words to Mr. Calder. Then he added one small stone and looked at his work. It was like putting together a puzzle.

"Mr. Smith?" said Mrs. Butterman.

He looked up, surprised. "Hello Mrs. Butterman. Can I help?" he asked.

"Is there a priest in town? Penny Cooper and Nate Tilden want to get married," said Ella Butterman.

"I think we do, now," he said. "We have a priest who is visiting from up-river. Father Mazzuchelli. Young man, very kind. He's Italian. But he speaks good English and a little German. He's starting a Catholic church over near the Land Office. We're having mass on Sundays, now."

Mr. Calder spoke up, "Yah? That is good to know. My wife wants to come. With our children. I'll tell her."

"Father Mazzuchelli should be here today. You might find him at the log cabin just next to the Land Office," said Mr. Smith. Then he turned back to his work. Where should he put the next stone?

Mr. Butterman rode Harv around Key City to find men to finish building the two houses. Some men who were mining lead wanted to find extra work. So he visited all the lead mines he knew about. Harv was happy to be out. He was a tall horse, and he got places pretty fast. With Harv, Mr. Butterman was able to visit ten mines in just two hours. To Mr. Butterman's surprise, he came upon Bowe, who had left Mr. Sweeney's place.

"What are you doing here?" said Mr. Butterman. "Mr. Sweeney is looking for you. He scared Mrs. Calder. He was pretty mad when you left with Tommy."

"Oh! I'm not worried 'bout Mr. Sweeney," said Bowe. "He knows I'm here. He told me if I wanted to mine lead, I could do it. I just have to give him a little of what I make. But so far, I'm not making anything. Not much lead here."

"I see," said Mr. Butterman. He

offered Bowe extra work building his two houses. So for a few weeks, Bowe walked from his lead mine and helped with the house building.

CHAPTER EIGHTEEN

Key City, Iowa Territory, July 10, 1834

It took several more weeks, but Mr. and Mrs. Butterman, Penny Cooper, Nate Tilden, and Aunt Sunday finally moved into their new houses. It was an early July Sunday afternoon when they finished moving in. The wedding was set for the following Sunday. Father Mazzuchelli, the priest, agreed to marry Nate and Penny. In one more week, they would be man and wife.

Penny and Nate went over to the Buttermans' house for dinner. It was a hot evening, even when the sun disappeared behind the bluff.

"It never seems to get dark this time

of year," Mrs. Butterman said. "What a change from last November, when the days were so short!"

It was so different than being at the log cabin at Calder Creek. Here in Key City they could hear other people talking all the time. And there were so many more houses. Penny couldn't believe it. There was even a new hotel just five minutes away. A lot of trees were cut down now. It was a big change from the first time Penny saw Key City. Last November it was just a collection of log cabins and buildings in a small clearing in an endless forest. Now there were large bare areas with houses and buildings on them. Penny could see almost all the way to the Mississippi River from where she stood.

She waved her hand at a few mosquitoes. She said to Ella Butterman, "We should go back to Calder Creek and see if any of our sweet potatoes are ready to dig up. With all these mosquitoes, mosquito fever will come. Eating sweet potatoes might help."

Mrs. Butterman agreed. They planned to visit the Buttermans' land on Calder Creek soon. "I've never cooked sweet potatoes," she said. "I hope Aunt Sunday can show me how."

"Where is she, anyway?" said Mr. Butterman. He looked up at the house behind them.

"She told me she has a toothache," said Mrs. Butterman. "I think she's resting in her new room."

Mr. Butterman asked Nate, "How

old do you think Aunt Sunday is?" Nate came from the same farm in Virginia. He might know.

"I'm not too sure," said Nate. "She was old when I was born. If I'm twenty-five now, then she must be at least eighty years old?"

"Goodness," said Mrs. Butterman. "That's a good old age." Aunt Sunday was in fact ninety-one years old. This was something Aunt Sunday herself didn't know.

"You know," said Jonathan Butterman, "There are so many people in Key City now. I think I might start a bank."

"A bank!" said Mrs. Butterman.

"Yes, a bank," Mr. Butterman answered. "Everyone still has to go back to Leadville to use the bank there. That means crossing the Mississippi River. Going all the way back to Illinois. The miners can sell their lead here. They can bank right here in Key City."

"The Butterman Bank?" said Mrs. Butterman.

"Well, maybe another name," said Mr. Butterman, laughing.

CHAPTER NINETEEN

Key City, Iowa Territory,
July 11, 1834

When Bowe came for work the next day, he found Mr. Butterman and Nate Tilden waiting for him. They had shovels. Mr. Butterman wanted to dig a water well behind his new house.

"We need a good place to get water," said Mr. Butterman. "Last summer I heard they had cholera. No one really knows where that comes from. But I think it's from drinking bad water. If we have a good water well, we might be alright."

Nate thought so, too. Cholera was a scary sickness. It killed a lot of people and always in summer. Maybe it came from bad water. Digging a new water well might help.

Nate said, "We're going to need more stones. After we dig down and find water, we'll need them to line the well. That'll keep the sides of the well from falling in."

"We have more stones on my land at Calder Creek," said Mr. Butterman. "We can bring back a wagonful by dinner time." Mr. Butterman left Bowe to start digging the water well. Mr. Butterman and Nate drove a wagon with two horses to Calder Creek. They loaded more stones and rocks onto the wagon until it was heavy and full. It was only two o'clock.

"That should be enough for now,"

said Mr. Butterman. "And anyway, I think it's going to storm. We should get back." Both men looked up at the sky. To the east toward the river the sky was blue and sunny. But to the west they could see dark clouds.

"Huh," said Nate. "We'd best get back. Make sure our windows are closed. It looks like rain, for sure."

Mr. Butterman and Nate Tilden drove the wagon as fast as they could. It was hard for the horses to pull so many rocks. And there wasn't really a road.

The clouds to the west became black. They moved slowly over the sky until it almost looked like night. And it was only the middle of the afternoon. There was a flash of light with a crack. Then a giant boom of thunder. It sounded like it was right overhead. The two horses tried to run. But Mr. Butterman held them back. They could get hurt pulling such a heavy wagon.

Nate pointed to his right. He shouted, "We can't make it back before this storm hits! Go up there, next to the bluff! See there! It's a lead mine! We can get out of the worst of the storm!"

Mr. Butterman saw the spot. He and Nate jumped off the wagon. They led the scared horses to the base of the bluff. There was less wind there. There were a few trees outside the small black entrance of the mine. A heavy rain began to fall. There was another crack of lightning and a boom of thunder. But it was moving to the east. As the two men watched the storm, two more men came up behind them. They were covered in dirt from the lead mine. Nate turned around first. Rick and Ed Ginn stood there. They were smiling. Rick Ginn was missing a front tooth. Mr. Butterman turned around and saw them, too. He looked hard at the Ginn brothers. He was ready for trouble if he had to be. But then a strange, loud sound came over the bluff. It was so loud the men could not think!

"Look at that! Look at that!" shouted Nate. Right overhead, in the black-green light of the storm, was a huge black cloud. It turned and turned and turned.

CHAPTER TWENTY

The Ginn brothers' lead mine, Iowa Territory, July 11, 1834

"Waugh!" shouted Mr. Butterman.

"Oh god!" shouted Ed Ginn. Then he laughed. And laughed. He pulled out his gun. Then he fired it right up into the sky, at the terrible turning black cloud. Both Nate Tilden and Jonathan Butterman looked at him like he was crazy. Ed Ginn *was* crazy.

Jonathan Butterman heard one of the horses scream. "Nate! Hold on to the horses! Don't let them run!" he shouted. They ran to Missy and Lap, who were both screaming by then. They were beyond scared. Nate could see the whites of their eyes. They never saw a tornado before. "Hold on now," he said to Missy. "Hold on. Tornado's moving away. Hold on."

The huge turning cloud was moving away. But it was still terrible to see. It was black and green. Lightning flashed all around it and inside it. It was like a huge animal.

It was still raining, but not so hard. But Mr. Butterman wanted to go. They couldn't stay with the Ginn brothers there. He didn't know what they would do. They hated Nate. And they stole horses.

"Come on," said Jonathan Butterman. "The storm's letting up. Let's get out of here."

They got on the wagon and made

their way back to the path to Key City. They heard the Ginn brothers laughing. One of them shouted, "Where you goin', Butterman?! Are you afraid of a little tornado?" The other shouted, "Nate! Hey Nate! Don't leave us!" More laughter.

Mr. Butterman shook his head. Then he said, "They know our names."

"Yeah," said Nate. "That's not good."

They rode slowly into Key City. The rain stopped. They could still see the black-green tornado turning and turning in the air. It was over the Mississippi River now. There were some trees down. No one seemed hurt. They saw one runaway horse. He was headed in the direction of the Ginn brothers.

"Whoever owns that horse, he'll never see it again. Those Ginn brothers will steal it!" said Nate. Both men laughed. But they were worried about what they would find at home in Key City. That was a bad storm. It had come up so fast.

When they got to the Buttermans' house in Key City, they found Mrs. Wheat and Miss Mallow. A tree fell on their building. One side of the building was gone. They ran out in the rain. Then they ran to the Buttermans' house. Mrs. Wheat was shaking. She was still scared. Mrs. Butterman gave her some hot tea. Mrs. Wheat could hardly lift the teacup to her lips.

"I never saw such a thing!" said Miss Mallow. "All black and green! Just turning and turning up in the sky!" She reached over to help her sister bring the teacup to her lips.

"Are you alright?" Mrs. Butterman asked Mr. Butterman.

"Yes," he answered. After a minute he said, "That tornado came right over the bluff. We didn't even see it coming." After another long minute he continued, "And we ran into the Ginn brothers. They have a lead mine right where we turn south from Calder Creek."

"Oh no," said Ella Butterman.

"Oh yes," said Mr. Butterman. "For a minute, I thought Ed Ginn was going crazy. He laughed at the storm. And he shot his gun at it! Then he laughed at us for getting out of there. It was worse than the tornado, to tell the truth."

"Well," said Mrs. Wheat. She looked less scared now after drinking some tea. "Now you know where Rick and Ed Ginn are. Just stay away from them. People turn up hurt or dead when those two men are around."

CHAPTER TWENTY-ONE

Key City, Iowa Territory,
July 17, 1834

One of the windows at the Buttermans' house was broken. But everything else seemed alright. Penny Cooper and Nate Tilden's house wasn't even touched. Penny and Nate started getting ready for their wedding. Penny sewed herself a new dress in light pink. And Nate found himself some dark pants and a clean white shirt. Mr. Butterman brought over two fat turkeys for the wedding dinner. Penny and Nate invited Jonathan and Ella Butterman, Aunt Sunday, Mrs. Wheat, Miss Mallow, James Smith, and Bowe and Tommy.

They also invited three newcomers, all of them dark-skinned, who hoped to live free in Iowa Territory. There was a lady named Caroline Bender, a man named Sam Walsh, and one other man named Walter Parker. Walter Parker was a barber. He cut Nate's hair. Nate would be ready for his wedding.

To Penny's surprise, Nate wanted to invite old Mr. Sweeney to the wedding!

"What?" she said. "Why would you invite *him*?"

Nate laughed. "After I doctored his horses, he changed how he talks to me. He listens and doesn't shout or get angry. Oh, he's still an angry, lonely old man. He'll never really like me. But it's a wedding. It's a happy time. Anyway, don't you want to give Alice and her two children a chance to come into Key City? Don't you think she's lonely all the time? Living up there on Calder Creek with just her kids and old Mr. Sweeney?"

Penny raised one shoulder, thinking. Then she nodded. "Alright," she said. "But you get to ask him." And so the next day Nate rode over to Mr. Sweeney's place and invited him. He was careful to ride far away from the Ginn brothers' lead mine.

On the day of the wedding a very light rain fell. For once it was cool. The wedding party met at Penny and Nate's house. From there they all walked to the small log cabin where Father Samuel Mazzuchelli waited for them. He was a tiny man. He was Italian. When he spoke English, it had the sound of singing in it. He had dark hair, and he wore the long black and white coat of a priest. He moved to meet them at the doorway of the cabin. He had a quick smile, and he held his arms open. "Welcome! Everyone welcome!" he said. "Let us marry this man and this woman in the eyes of God!" He shook hands with everyone in the wedding party. He even shook hands with Mr. Sweeney, who said, "I never met a priest from Italy before."

Father Mazzuchelli laughed. But then with warm eyes and a quiet voice he said, "You are welcome in this church. I welcome you, and God welcomes you! It's not much yet. But next year we build a real church. A beautiful place! A place for God's people to meet." Mr. Sweeney turned red. But he seemed pleased.

Everyone went into the small log cabin. At the back of the cabin was a table. The table had a beautiful white cloth. A small gold cross sat in the middle of the cloth. Penny felt a feeling, a little like she was going to cross the Mississippi River again. She was excited and scared. But she knew once she crossed this river, her life would be completely different. Standing there in her pink dress, she knew she would never go back. She would not leave Iowa. And she would be Nate's wife.

"You look beautiful," said Nate. He took her hand.

Father Mazzuchelli said in his singing English, "We have come rejoicing into the house of the Lord for this celebration, dear brothers and sisters, and now we stand with Penny and Nate." And so the wedding began.

AUTHOR'S NOTE

This story is about my hometown. It has another name. But it was also called "The Key City" many years ago. As a teenager in high school, I heard a strange story from a schoolmate. She said that African American slaves lived in Key City in the very early days of the city. In fact, African Americans lived on the land where her house was. It was true her house was very old. It dated from the 1840s. I always remembered that story. What were people's lives like in the early days of the city? Why were the African Americans such a secret? I lived in Key City for twenty years. But I never heard anyone else talk about that part of the history of the city. There were no lessons on enslaved people at school. Key City was in the northern United States. I never thought enslaved people would live in the North. But of course, the truth is not always what we think it is. It is better and it is worse.

There were in fact African American and American Indian slaves in Illinois, Iowa, Wisconsin, and Minnesota as late as the 1840s. It was something hidden, even at that time. Some who owned slaves simply said they were "servants." When it appeared that Iowa Territory would finally move against owning slaves, some slave owners quietly moved their slaves across the state line into Missouri. Slavery was allowed in Missouri and many other Southern states until the Civil War in the 1860s. When Iowa became a state in 1846 it was moving in the direction of becoming a free state. By 1849 it was against the law to hold any non-white person against their will in Iowa. This does not mean, however, that African Americans had an easy time of it in Iowa.

This is a story. It is fiction. Where I could, I found facts from histories of my hometown. I also learned about real individuals in early Key City who lived there in the 1830s. One of them, James Smith, was the great-great-great-great-grandfather of my childhood babysitter, Michelle (thank you, Michelle!). And Mr. Smith was indeed a stone mason. Father Samuel Charles Mazzuchelli was a priest and missionary on the Illinois, Iowa, and Wisconsin frontier. He created the foundation for the Roman

Catholic faith in that area. He died in Benton, Wisconsin, in 1864 after caring for a sick church member. Today, his grave and his church can be seen in Google Maps photographs of the town. As you can see for yourself, his grave is covered by beautiful red geraniums. Other details I made up by guessing as best I could what people might have thought or said so many years ago. It was a different world. Whatever mistakes I made are mine.

My sources were:

Bennet, Mary, and Paul Juhl. *Iowa Stereographs: Three-Dimensional Visions of the Past.* Iowa City: University of Iowa Press, 1997.

Davis, Ronald L. F. *The Black Experience*

in Natchez, 1720–1880: A Special History Study. Natchez: Natchez National Historical Park, 1994.

Dykstra, Robert. *Bright Radical Star: Black Freedom and White Supremacy on the Hawkeye Frontier*. Cambridge: Harvard University Press, 1993.

Lillie, Robin M., and Jennifer E. Mack. *Dubuque's Forgotten Cemetery: Excavating a Nineteenth-Century Burial Ground in a Twenty-first Century City*. Iowa City: University of Iowa Press, 2015.

Schwalm, Leslie A. *Emancipation's Diaspora: Race and Reconstruction in the Upper Midwest*. Chapel Hill: The University of North Carolina Press, 2009.

Thanks to Anthony Jahn, State Archivist, State Historical Society of Iowa, for his timely assistance. Thanks also to the editors for their eye for detail.

CPSIA information can be obtained
at www.ICGtesting.com
Printed in the USA
BVHW031521310319
544170BV00001B/58/P